Wee Sing®

BIBLE SONGS

By
Pamela Conn Beall and
Susan Hagen Nipp

Illustrated by
Nancy Spence Klein

PSSI
PRICE STERN SLOAN

To Life

Special thanks to our Wee Singers: Hilary Beall, Kyle
Beall, Lindsay Beall, Ryan Nipp, Devin Nipp, Sam Klein,
Erin Klein, Katie Klein, Rachel Macy,
Peter Macy and John Macy. . . .

And to our musical producers
Barry Hagen and Mauri Macy

2005 Edition
Cover illustration copyright © by Liisa Chauncy Guida

PREFACE

Sing unto God, sing praises to His name
Psalm 68:4
I will sing praises unto the Lord
Psalm 27:6

Just as David in the Psalms writes of singing praises to God, we continue to sing of God's glory in our contemporary world.

In *Wee Sing Bible Songs,* we have collected mainly traditional songs of unknown origin that children have loved for years. They tell of Bible heroes, teachings, parables, praises and prayers with many of their lyrics being directly related to specific passages of the Bible. We have noted these Scripture verses above the music so you can refer to them and more fully understand the background of the song.

A selection of spirituals has been omitted because we previously published them in *Wee Sing Around the Campfire.* In that book you will find "Oh When the Saints," "Joshua Fought the Battle," "Get on Board Little Children," "Heav'n, Heav'n," "Nobody Knows the Trouble I've Seen," "Jacob's Ladder," "Swing Low," "Rocka My Soul," "One More River" and the full story of "Rise and Shine."

Whether you are memorizing the books of the Bible through song, singing the story of David and Goliath or lifting your voice in praise, we hope you enjoy the gift that God has given us all – – – – music.

Pam Beall
Susan Nipp

TABLE OF CONTENTS

The Bible Says

*Titles with asterisks are fingerplays which are rhymes illustrated by the use of finger motions.

We Praise and Pray

The Bible Says

JESUS LOVES THE LITTLE CHILDREN

C.H. Woolston
George F. Root

Je-sus loves the lit-tle chil-dren,

All the chil-dren of the world, Red and

yel-low, black and white, They are pre-cious in His

sight, Je-sus loves the lit-tle chil-dren of the world.

JESUS LOVES ME

Anna B. Warner, Mark 10:14   Wm. B. Bradbury

7

JESUS LOVES EVEN ME

PPB

Philip P. Bliss

I am so glad that Je-sus loves me,
Je-sus loves me, Je-sus loves me, I am so glad that
Je-sus loves me, Je-sus loves e-ven me.—

*Guitar play in key of E (E, A, B⁷)

JESUS SEES ME

Jesus sees me when I sleep,
  (rest head on hands)

Jesus sees me when I play,
  (turn around)

Jesus sees me all the time,
  (arms outstretched)

And he cares for me each day.
  (cross arms over chest)

Suggestion:
Can be sung to the tune "Jesus Loves Me"

8

COME BLESS THE LORD

Psalm 134:1,2

Come bless the Lord, (Come bless the Lord,) all ye

ser-vants of the Lord, (all ye ser-vants of the

Lord,) who stand by night (who stand by night) in the

house of the Lord, (in the house of the Lord) Lift

up your hands (Lift up your hands) in the

ho-ly place, (in the ho-ly place,) And

bless the Lord, (And bless the Lord) and

bless the Lord. (and bless the Lord)

9

JESUS WANTS ME FOR A SUNBEAM

Nellie Talbot
Matthew 5:16

E.O. Excell

Je-sus wants me for a sun-beam, To shine for Him each day, In ev-'ry way try to please Him, At home, at school, at play.

chorus

A sun-beam, a sun-beam, Je-sus wants me for a sun-beam, A sun-beam, a sun-beam, I'll be a sun-beam for Him.—

THIS LITTLE LIGHT OF MINE

Matthew 5:15-16

1. This lit-tle light of mine, I'm gon-na let it shine,
This lit-tle light of mine, I'm gon-na let it shine, let it
shine, let it shine, let it shine.

2. [b]Hide it under a bushel? [c]NO!
   [a]I'm gonna let it shine.
   [b]Hide it under a bushel? [c]NO!
   [a]I'm gonna let it shine, let it shine,
   let it shine, let it shine.
3. [a]Don't let Satan [d]blow it out,
   [a]I'm gonna let it shine,
   [a]Don't let Satan [d]blow it out,
   [a]I'm gonna let it shine, let it shine,
   let it shine, let it shine.
4. Repeat verse 1

Actions:
a) hold up left forefinger throughout verse   b) cover finger with right palm   c) shout
"NO" and uncover finger   d) blow at top of finger instead of singing "blow"

THE BIBLE SAYS

The Bible says that Jesus
   (hands form book)

Was loving, kind and good,
   (cross arms on chest)

I want to live as Jesus did
   (point to self)

And do the things I should.
   (nod head)

THE LORD IS MY SHEPHERD
(Round)

Psalm 23

The Lord is my—shep-herd, I'll walk with Him al-way.

He knows me and He loves me, I'll walk with Him al-way.

Al-way, al-way, I'll walk with Him al-way.

Al-way, al-way, I'll walk with Him al-way.

DEEP AND WIDE

Psalm 36:9

1. Deep and wide, deep and wide, There's a foun-tain flow-ing deep and wide. Deep and wide, deep and wide, There's a foun-tain flow-ing deep and wide.

2. Repeat song leaving out "deep" but do action
3. Repeat song leaving out "deep" and "wide" but do actions
4. Repeat song leaving out "deep," "wide" and "fountain," but do actions

Actions:
a) hands measure deep   b) hands measure wide   c) wiggle fingers left to right

* Guitar play in key of A (A, D, E⁷)

13

GOD MADE ME

1. (a)God made (b)me, (a)God made (b)me,
(c)In my Bi-ble-Book it says that (a)God made (b)me.

2. (a)God loves (b)me, (a)God loves (b)me,
   (c)In my Bible Book it says that
   (a)God loves (b)me.
3. (a)God helps (b)me...
4. (a)God keeps (b)me...

Actions:
a) point up   b) point to self
c) hands form book

MY BODY, STRONG AND GOOD

I have two eyes that wink and blink,
   I have a mind to make me think,
I have two hands that clap for fun,
   I have two feet that jump and run,
I have two ears to hear a song,
   Two lips to praise Him all day long,
I have a body strong and good,
   To use for Jesus as I should.

Actions:
Point to body parts and do as words suggest.

14

OH, BE CAREFUL
(Tune: If You're Happy)

1. Oh, be care-ful lit-tle eyes what you see,
Oh, be care-ful lit-tle eyes what you see,
For the Fa-ther up a-bove is look-ing down in love,
So be care-ful lit-tle eyes what you see.

2. Oh, be ᵈcareful little ears what you hear,
    Oh, be ᵈcareful little ears what you hear,
For the ᵇFather up above is ᶜlooking down in love,
    So be ᵈcareful little ears what you hear.

3. Oh, be ᵉcareful little hands what you do...

4. Oh, be ᶠcareful little feet where you go...

5. Oh, be ᵍcareful little heart whom you trust...

6. Oh, be ʰcareful little mind what you think...

Actions:
a) point to eyes   b) point up   c) shade eyes   d) cup hands around ears
e) hold out hands   f) point to feet   g) hands over heart   h) point to temple

* Guitar play in key of E (E, A, B⁷)

15

SILVER AND GOLD HAVE I NONE

Acts 3:1-8

Pe-ter and John went to pray;—They met a lame man on the way, He asked for alms — and held out his palms and this is what Pe-ter did say:—"Sil-ver and gold have I none,— but such as I have give I thee, In the name of Je — sus Christ— of Naz-a-reth, rise up and walk." He went walk-ing and leap-ing and prais-ing God, walk-ing and leap-ing and

prais-ing God, "In the name of Je—sus
Christ—— of Naz-a-reth, rise up and walk."

THE TWELVE DISCIPLES

Peter, Andrew, James and John,
  Fishermen of Capernaum,
Thomas and St. Matthew, too,
  Philip and Bartholomew,
James, his brother Thaddeus,
  Simon, and the one named Judas,
Twelve disciples here in all,
  Following the Master's call.

17

BEHOLD, BEHOLD

Revelations 3:20

Be-hold, be-hold! I stand at the door and

Knock, Knock, Knock; Be-hold, be-hold! I

stand at the door and knock, Knock, Knock; If

an-y-one hear my voice, If an-y-one hear my voice,

and will o-pen, o-pen, o-pen the door, I will come in

Actions:
a) knock three times   b) right hand cup ear   c) left hand cup ear   d) hands measure narrow   e) hands wider apart   f) hands even wider apart   g) hands over heart

* Guitar play in key of A (A, D, E, E⁷, B⁷)

ONE DOOR AND ONLY ONE

One door and on-ly one, And yet its sides are two,

In-side and out-side, On which side are you?

One door and on-ly one, And yet its sides are two,

I'm on the in-side, On which side are you?

Actions:
a) hold up forefinger   b) hold up two fingers   c) hold up hand, palm facing in
d) palm facing out   e) point out   f) point to self

*Guitar play in key of E (E, A, B^7, F)

LOVE, LOVE
(Round)

Leviticus 19:18

Love, love, love, love, Chris-tians this

is your — call, Love your neigh-bor

as your — self, For God loves — all.

19

THIS IS MY COMMANDMENT

MVF, *John 15:12*

Marvin V. Frey

THE B-I-B-L-E

The B - I - B - L - E , yes, that's the

book for me, I@stand a - lone on the

Word of God, The B - I - B - L - E.

Optional Descant

S.N.

The B-I-B-L-E, yes, that's the book for me, I

@stand a - lone,— The B - I - B - L - E.

Action:
a) stand up

Suggestion:
Make a large card for each of the letters of B-I-B-L-E. Five children hold
the cards. As word is spelled, child holds letter above head. Hold in
front of chest for other lyrics.

BOOKS OF THE OLD TESTAMENT

Susan Nipp

Gen-e-sis, Ex-o-dus, Le-vi-ti-cus, Num-bers, Deu-ter-on-o-

my, Josh-ua, Judg-es, Ruth,— First and Se-cond Sam-uel,

First Kings, Sec-ond Kings, First and Sec-ond Chron-i-cles,

Ez-ra, Ne-he-mi—ah, Es-ther, Job, Psalms, Pro—verbs, Ec-

cle-si-as-tes , Song of Sol-o-mon, I-sai-ah, Jer-e-mi-ah,

Lam-en-ta-tions, E-ze-kiel, Dan-iel, Ho-se-a, Joel, A-mos, O-ba-

di-ah, Jo-nah, Mi-cah, Na—hum, Ha-bak-kuk, Zeph-an-

i—ah, Hag-ga-i, Zech-a-ri-ah, and the last book Mal-a-chi.

22

BOOKS OF THE NEW TESTAMENT

Susan Nipp

Mat-thew, Mark, Luke and John, Acts and the

let-ter to the Ro-mans, First and Sec-ond Cor-

in-thi-ans, Ga-la-tians and E-phe-sians, Phil-ip-pi-

ans, Col-os-sians, First and Sec-ond Thes-sa-lo-nians,

First and Sec-ond Tim-o-thy, Ti-tus and Phi-le-mon,

He-brews and the book of James, First and Se-cond

Pe-ter, First and Se-cond, Third — John,

Jude and Rev-e-la-tion.

FATHER ABRAHAM

1. Fa-ther Ab-ra-ham had man-y sons, man-y sons had Fa-ther Ab-ra-ham, I am one of them and so are you, so let's all praise the Lord. Right arm!

2. Father Abraham had many sons,
   Many sons had Father Abraham,
   I am one of them and so are you,
   So let's all praise the Lord.
   [a]Right arm, [b]left arm!

3. Father Abraham...
   [a]Right arm, [b]left arm, [c]right foot!

4. ... [d]left foot!

5. ... [e]chin up!

6. ... [f]turn around!

7. ... [g]sit down!

Actions:
a) clench fist, bend and extend arm upward repeatedly throughout song   b) add left arm in same motion as right   c) add right foot stepping up and down   d) add left foot stepping up and down   e) add head nodding up and down f) add turning in place while continuing other motions g) sit down

24

LITTLE DAVID, PLAY ON YOUR HARP

Spiritual

Lit-tle Da-vid play on your harp, Hal-le-
lu, hal-le-lu, Lit-tle Da-vid play on your
harp, Hal-le-lu. — Lit-tle Da-vid play on your
harp, Hal-le-lu, hal-le-lu, Lit-tle Da-vid
play on your harp, Hal-le-lu. —

Lit-tle Da-vid was a shep-herd boy, He
Killed Go-li-ath and shout-ed for joy. —

25

ONLY A BOY NAMED DAVID

A.A.
I Samuel 17:49

Arthur Arnott

(h)in the sling, And the (b)sling went round and round; And round and round and round and round, And round and round and round, And (g)one lit-tle stone went (i)up in the air, And the gi-ant came tum-bling (j)down.

Actions:
a) hand in front, palm down as in measuring   b) circle hand above head   c) hands in prayer position   d) hands around mouth   e) wiggle fingers left to right   f) hold up five fingers   g) hold up forefinger   h) put finger into palm of opposite hand   i) shoot forefinger upward   j) fall down or clap

WHO DID SWALLOW JONAH?

1. Who did, who did, Who did, who did, Who did swal-low Jo, Jo, Jo, Jo, Who did, who did, Who did, who did, Who did swal-low Jo, Jo, Jo, Jo, Who did, who did, Who did, who did, Who did swal-low Jo, Jo, Jo, Jo, Who did swal-low Jo-nah, who did swal-low Jo-nah, Who did swal-low Jo-nah down? —

2. Whale did...swallow Jo, Jo, Jo, Jo... (3 times)
   Whale did swallow Jonah...down.
3. Gabriel...blow your trum, trum, trum, trum...
   Gabriel blow your trumpet...loud.
4. Noah...in the arky, arky...
   Noah in the arky...bailed.
5. Daniel...in the li, li, li, li...
   Daniel in the lion's...den.
6. Peter...on the sea, sea, sea, sea...
   Peter walking on the...sea.

28

ZACCHAEUS

Luke 19:1-5

Actions:
a) hands in front, right palm raised above left palm as in measuring   b) palms closer   c) alternate hands as if climbing   d) shade eyes, look down   e) swing arms as in walking   f) shade eyes, look up   g) beckon with hand   h) clap in rhythm

29

THE WISE MAN AND FOOLISH MAN

Matthew 7:24-27

1. The wise man built his house up-on the rock,

The wise man built his house up-on the rock,

The wise man built his house up-on the rock,

And the rains came tum-bling down.

Chorus

The rains came down and the floods came up,

30

The rains came down and the floods came up,

The rains came down and the floods came up,

And the house on the rock stood firm.

2. The foolish man built his house upon the sand,
   The foolish man built his house upon the sand,
   The foolish man built his house upon the sand,
   And the rains came tumbling down.

Chorus:
   The rains came down and the floods came up,
   The rains came down and the floods came up,
   The rains came down and the floods came up,
   And the house on the sand went SMASH!

Actions:
a) pound one fist on top of the other in rhythm   b) wiggle fingers while moving hands downward   c) palms up, raise hands in rhythm   d) fingertips form rooftop
e) pound fists once   f) pound fist into open palm in rhythm   g) slap palms loudly

WHO BUILT THE ARK?

Genesis 6, 7   *Spiritual*

(Chorus F Solo) ... (C7 Group)

Who built the ark? No-ah! No-ah!

F Solo ... Group C7 ... F Fine

Who built the ark? Broth-er No-ah built the ark.

C. Solo

1. Old man No-ah built the ark, He built it out of the

G7 ... C

hick-o-ry bark. He built it long, both wide and tall

G7 ... C D.C.al Fine

With plen-ty of room for the large—and small.

2. In came the animals, two by two,
   Hippopotamus and kangaroo.
   In came the animals, three by three,
   Two big cats and a bumblebee.
       Chorus
3. In came the animals, four by four,
   Two through the window and two through the door.
   In came the animals, five by five,
   The bees came swarming from the hive.
       Chorus
4. In came the animals, six by six,
   Elephant laughed at the monkey's tricks.
   In came the animals, seven by seven,
   Giraffes and the camels looking up to heaven.
       Chorus
5. In came the animals, eight by eight,
   Some on time and the others were late.
   In came the animals, nine by nine,
   Some were laughin' and some were cryin'.
       Chorus
6. In came the animals, ten by ten,
   Time for the voyage to begin.
   Noah said, "Go shut the door,
   The rain's started fallin' and we can't take more."
       Chorus

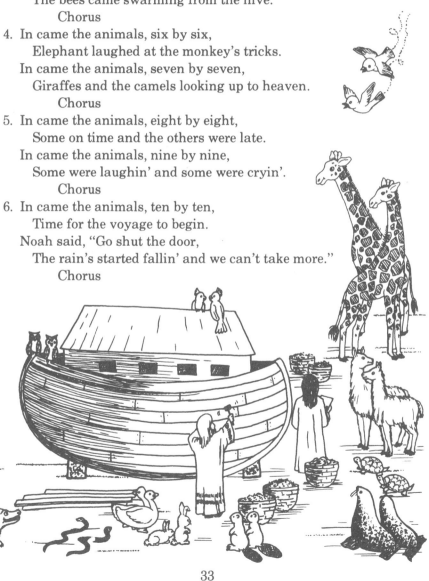

HIS BANNER OVER ME IS LOVE

Song of Solomon 2:4, 16

B.C. Laurelton

1. The Lord is mine and I am His,— His ban-ner o-ver me is love,— The Lord is mine and I am His,— His ban-ner o-ver me is love,— The Lord is mine and I am His,— His ban-ner o-ver me is love,— His ban-ner o-ver me — is love.—

2. He brought me to His banqueting table,
   His banner over me is love...) 3 times
   His banner over me is love.

3. He is the vine and we are the branches...

4. Jesus is the rock of my salvation...

Suggestion:

For younger children, use only verse 1 with these actions:

Actions:
a) point up   b) point to self   c) fingertips together over head   d) cross arms over chest

We Praise and Pray

PRAISE HIM, PRAISE HIM

@ 1. Praise Him, praise Him, all ye lit-tle chil-dren, God is love, God is love, Praise Him, praise Him, all ye lit-tle chil-dren, God is love, God is love.

2. [b]Love Him, love Him, all ye little children,
   God is love, God is love,
   Love Him, love Him, all ye little children,
   God is love, God is love.
3. [c]Thank Him, thank Him...
4. [d]Serve Him, serve Him...

Actions:
a) clap entire verse in rhythm   b) cross arms over chest   c) hands in prayer position   d) hands out front, palms up

KUM BA YAH

MVF　(Translation: Come By Here)　*Marvin V. Frey*

1. Kum ba yah, my Lord, Kum ba yah, Kum ba yah, my Lord, Kum ba yah: Kum ba yah, my Lord, Kum ba yah! Oh, Lord, — Kum ba yah!

2. [f]Someone's crying, [d]Lord, [a]Kum ba [b]yah,
3. [g]Someone's laughing, [d]Lord...
4. [h]Someone's singing, [d]Lord...
5. [i]Someone's praying, [d]Lord...
6. [a]Kum ba [b]yah [c]my [d]Lord...

Actions:
a) roll hands   b) hands outstretched   c) point to self   d) point up   e) thumb and forefinger form circle   f) wipe eyes   g) forefingers to corners of mouth to show smile   h) cup hands around mouth   i) hands in praying position

This version of "Come By Here" first appeared in "Revival Choruses of Marvin V. Frey," a lyric sheet printed in 1939 in Portland, Oregon. The chorus made its way to Africa with missionaries, and in 1948 the song returned from Africa with the translation of "Kum Ba Yah."

THANK YOU

Thank you for the world so sweet,
Thank you for the food we eat,
Thank you for the birds that sing,
Thank you, God, for everything.

WHISPER A PRAYER

1. Whis-per a pray'r in the morn-ing, Whis-per a

pray'r at noon,——— Whis-per a pray'r in the

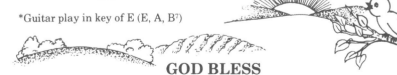

eve-ning, To keep——your heart in tune.——

2. God answers pray'r in the morning,
   God answers pray'r at noon,
   God answers pray'r in the evening,
   He'll keep your heart in tune.

*Guitar play in key of E (E, A, B⁷)

GOD BLESS

God bless all those that I love,
   God bless all those that love me,
God bless all those that love those that I love,
   And all those that love those that love me.

37

GIVE ME OIL IN MY LAMP

A. Sevison

Give me oil in my lamp, Keep me burn-ing, (burn-ing, burn-ing,) Give me oil in my lamp, I pray, (Hal-le-lu-ia) Give me oil in my lamp, Keep me burn-ing, (burn-ing, burn-ing,) Keep me burn-ing 'til the break of day.

Sing "Ho-san-na", sing "Ho-san-na," Sing "Ho-san-na to the King of Kings,"

Sing "Ho-san-na," sing "Ho-san-na,"

Sing "Ho-san-na to the King."

Suggestion:
Divide into two groups. Group one sings verse and chorus without words in parentheses. Group two sings with group one on verse but adds words in parentheses. On chorus, group two sings descant of whole notes.

ISN'T HE WONDERFUL

MVF   *Marvin V. Frey*

Is-n't He won-der-ful, won-der-ful, won-der-ful,

Is-n't Je-sus, my Lord, won-der-ful! Eyes have

seen, ears have heard, It's re-cord-ed in God's

word. Is-n't Je-sus, my Lord, won-der-ful!

Actions:
a) clap in rhythm   b) hand shade eyes   c) hand cup ear   d) hands form book

Composed 1947. Copyright © 1973 by Marvin V. Frey.
All rights reserved. Used by permission.

STANDIN' IN THE NEED OF PRAYER

Spiritual

2. Not my mother, not my father, but it's me, oh Lord,) 2 times
   Standin' in the need of pray'r...
        Chorus

3. Not the preacher, not the deacon... Chorus

4. Not my neighbor, not a stranger... Chorus

HE'S GOT THE WHOLE WORLD

1. He's got the whole world – in His hands, He's got the whole world – in His hands, He's got the whole world – in His hands, He's got the whole world in His hands.

2. He's got the little, bitty baby in His hands,
   He's got the little, bitty baby in His hands,
   He's got the little, bitty baby in His hands,
   He's got the whole world in His hands.

3. He's got you and me brother...
4. He's got you and me sister...
5. He's got everybody here...
6. He's got the wind and the rain...
7. He's got the sun and the moon...
8. He's got the whole world...

V. 1 Everett George Washington
V. 2 Marvin V. Frey

DO LORD

Spiritual

Verse G

1. I've got a home in glo-ry land that

(clap) out-shines the sun, (Oh, Lord-y,)

C

I've got a home in glo-ry land that

G

(clap) out-shines the sun. I've got a home in

glo-ry land that (clap) out-shines the

D7   G

sun, Look a-way be-yond—the blue.—

Chorus

Do Lord, oh, do Lord, oh, do re-mem-ber

C

me,(Oh,Lord-y) Do Lord, oh, do Lord, oh, do re-mem-ber

me, Do Lord, oh, do Lord, oh, do re - mem - ber

me, Look a - way be - yond — the blue. —

2. I took Jesus as my Savior,
   (clap) You take Him, too, (Oh, Lordy),
   I took Jesus as my Savior,
   (clap) You take Him, too,
   I took Jesus as my Savior,
   (clap) You take Him, too,
   Look away beyond the blue.
        Chorus

HERE IS THE CHURCH

Here is the church,
   (fold hands, fingers inside)
And here is the steeple,
   (index fingers up)
Open the doors,
   (thumbs apart)
And see all the people.
   (wiggle inside fingers)
Close the doors,
   (thumbs together)
And hear them pray,
   (hands to ear)
Open the doors,
   (thumbs apart)
And they all walk away.
   (fingers walk away)

CLIMB, CLIMB UP SUNSHINE MOUNTAIN

(a) Climb, climb up sun-shine moun-tain,
(b) Heav'n-ly breez-es blow, (a) Climb, climb up
sun-shine moun-tain, (c) Fac-es all a-glow,
(d) Turn, turn your face from doubt-ing,
(e) Look up in the sky, (a) Climb, climb up
sun-shine moun-tain, (f) you and (g) I.

Actions:
a) alternate hands as in climbing   b) wave hands from left to right   c) hands on either side of face   d) look to right   e) look up   f) point out   g) point to self

44

HEAVENLY SUNSHINE

H.J. Zelley

George W. Cooke

Heav-en-ly sun-shine, heav-en-ly sun-shine,

Flood-ing my soul with glo-ry di-vine,—

Heav-en-ly sun-shine, heav-en-ly sun-shine,

Hal - le - lu - jah, Je -sus is mine.

PRAISE THE LORD TOGETHER
(Round)

Praise the Lord to-geth-er sing-ing,

"Al-le-lu-ia, al-le-lu-ia, al-le-lu-ia".

RHC **MY GOD IS SO GREAT** *Ruth Harms Calkin*
Adapted

ⓐ My God is so great, so strong and so might-y! There's

ⓑ noth-ing my God can-not do! (clap, clap) My

ⓐ God is so great, so strong and so might-y! There's

ⓑ noth-ing my God can-not do! (clap, clap) The

ⓒ moun-tains are His, ⓓ the riv-ers are His, The

ⓔ stars are His hand-i-work too, —— My

*Guitar play in Key of E (E, A, B⁷)

46

God is so great, so strong and so might-y! There's

noth-ing my God can-not do! For you!

Actions:
a) hold up arms and flex muscles b) shake head "no" c) hands form mountain peak above head d) wiggle fingers from left to right e) fingers make twinkling stars f) point out

SEE THE CAMEL

See the camel, big and humpy,
  (bend over, hands on knees)

See the elephant walk so clumpy,
  (bend over, clasp hands and swing "trunk")

See the turtle, round and slow,
  (squat down, make circle with arms in front of body)

God made them that way, you know.
  (stand and point finger up)

See the squeaky mouse so small,
  (crouch down, bend elbows, make little paws with hands)

Different from the horse that's tall,
  (reach high on tiptoe)

See the robin flap his wings,
  (flap arms)

Thank you, God, who made all things.
  (bow head, fold hands in prayer)

PEACE LIKE A RIVER

MVF   *Marvin V. Frey*

1. I've got peace like a riv-er, I've got peace like a riv-er, I've got peace like a riv-er in my soul. —

I've got peace like a riv-er, I've got peace like a riv-er, I've got peace like a riv-er in my soul. —

2. I've got joy like a fountain...
3. I've got love like an ocean...

Composed 1951. Copyright © 1974 by Marvin V. Frey.
All rights reserved. Used by permission.

Optional Descant

S. N.

I've got peace, — I've got peace, — I've got peace — in my soul. — I've got peace, — I've got peace, — I've got peace — in my soul.

WALKING WITH JESUS

Walk-ing with Je-sus, Walk-ing ev'-ry day,

All a-long the way, for I am walk-ing with

Je-sus, Walk-ing with Je-sus a-lone.

Optional Descant

Walk-ing in the sun-light, Walk-ing in the sha-dow,

Suggestion:
Divide into two groups. Group one sing song as written. Group two sing descant where marked with brackets. Join group one on remaining measures.

* Guitar play in key of E (E, A, B⁷)

49

NOW I LAY

Now I lay me down to sleep,
I pray the Lord my soul to keep,
Thy love be with me through the night,
And keep me til the morning light.

FATHER, WE THANK THEE

Rebecca J. Weston   *Daniel Batchellor*

Fa-ther, we thank Thee for the — night,

And for the pleas-ant morn — ing — light,

For rest and food and lov-ing — care,

And all that makes the — world so — fair.

GOD IS SO GOOD

1. God is so good, God is so good,
God is so good, He's so good to me.

2. God loves me so, God loves me so,
    God loves me so, He's so good to me.

3. God answers prayer...

Optional Descant

S.N.

God — is so good to me, God — is so good,

God — is so good to me, so good to — me.

I'M IN THE LORD'S ARMY

ⓐ I may nev-er march in the in-fan-try,

ⓑ Ride in the cav-al-ry, © Shoot in the ar-til-ler-y,

ⓓ I may nev-er fly o'er the en-e-my, But

ⓔ I'm in the Lord's ar-my. ⓕ (yes sir!)

ⓔ I'm in the Lord's ar-my, ⓕ (yes sir!)

ⓐ I'm in the Lord's ar-my, ⓕ (yes sir!)

Actions:
a) march in place   b) hold reins, bounce as riding horse   c) clap once at shoulder
height, sliding one hand forward, one back   d) arms out as an airplane   e) hand to
brow in a salute   f) extend arm and return to salute in rhythm

52

HAPPY ALL THE TIME

I'm (a) in-right, (b) out-right, (c) up-right, (d) down-right

(e) hap-py all the time, I'm (a) in-right, (b) out-right,

(c) up-right, (d) down-right (e) hap-py all the time. Since

(f) Je-sus Christ came (g) in and (h) cleansed my

heart from sin, I'm (a) in-right, (b) out-right,

(c) up-right, (d) down-right (e) hap-py all the time.

Actions:
a) point to chest   b) point out   c) point up   d) point down   e) clap hands
f) arms up   g) point to chest with both hands   h) draw heart in air with both hands

GOD'S LOVE

M.M.

Mauri Macy

Chorus C

So I nev-er will for-get,— I sing a lit-tle song
and this song al-ways re-minds me that God loves—
me, And it's al-ways bet-ter yet—when some-one
sings a-long— So two of us—can know a-bout-God's love.

Verse G7

1. He made pup-py dogs— pup-py dogs— to
run and play with me and Kit-ty cats,—
Kit-ty cats— as soft and warm can be,—

2. He made dairy cows, dairy cows to give us chocolate shakes,
   And dish rags, dish rags to clean the mess we make.   Chorus
3. He made sunshine, sunshine to warm the winter air,
   And woolly sheep, woolly sheep to give us clothes to wear. Chorus

Frederick Whitfield **OH, HOW I LOVE JESUS**

Oh, how I love Je - sus, Oh, how I love

Je - sus, — Oh, how I love Je - sus, be-

cause —— He first loved me. —

Part 2

To me, He is so won - der - ful and I

love — Him, To me, He is so won - der - ful and I

love — Him, To me, He is so won - der - ful and I

love — Him, be - cause — He first loved me.

HALLELU, HALLELU

Hal-le-lu, hal-le-lu, hal-le-lu, hal-le-lu-jah! Praise ye the Lord! Hal-le-lu, hal-le-lu, hal-le-lu, hal-le-lu-jah! Praise ye the Lord! Praise ye the Lord, hal-le-lu-jah! Praise ye the Lord, hal-le-lu-jah! Praise ye the Lord, hal-le-lu-jah! Praise ye the Lord!

Suggestion:
Divide into two groups. Group 1 stand and sing on all the "Hallelus." Group 2 stand and sing on all the "Praise Ye the Lords." Sit when not singing.

OUR HANDS WE FOLD

Our hands we fold,
Our heads we bow,
For food and drink
We thank Thee now.

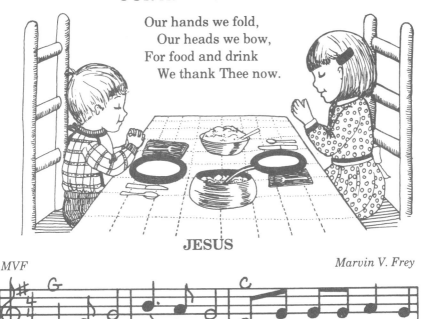

JESUS

MVF

Marvin V. Frey

1. Je — sus, Je — sus, Je - sus in the morn-ing,
Je - sus at the noon-time, Je — sus, Je — sus,
Je - sus when the sun goes down.

2. Praise Him, praise Him,
   Praise Him in the morning, praise Him at the noontime,
   Praise Him, praise Him,
   Praise Him when the sun goes down.

3. Love Him...

4. Serve Him...

5. Thank Him...

I LOVE TO TAKE A WALK

How I love to take a walk a-long the street,

And to say, "Hel-lo," to the peo-ple that I meet,

And to watch the show of their hap-py, hap-py feet,

And I say to my-self, It's a mir-a-cle.

Hal-le-lu, Hal—le-lu-ia! I sing as I walk a-

long, Hal-le-lu, Hal—le-lu-ia,

God has giv-en me such a hap-py, hap-py song,

THE WIND TELLS ME

The wind tells me,
  (sway like a tree in the wind)
The birds tell me,
  (flap arms)
The Bible tells me, too,
  (hands form book)
How much our Father loves us all,
  (arms outstretched)
And now I'm telling you.
  (point to self)   (point out)

RISE AND SHINE

Spiritual

(a) Rise — and (b) shine — and (c) give God the glo-ry, glo-ry,

(a) Rise — and (b) shine — and (c) give God the glo-ry, glo-ry,

(a) Rise and (b) shine and (clap) (c) give God the glo-ry, glo-ry,

(d) chil - dren of the Lord.

Actions:
a) hands in front, palms up and lift   b) hands outstretched on both sides of face
c) with hands still at sides of face, move upper body side to side in rhythm   d) clap in
rhythm to end of phrase

59

DOWN IN MY HEART

GWC

George W. Cooke

1. I have the joy, joy, joy, joy down in my

heart, (where?) Down in my heart, (where?)

down in my heart, I have the joy, joy,

joy, joy down in my heart, (where?)

Down in my heart to stay. And I'm so

*Guitar play in key of A (A, D, E⁷)

hap-py, so ver-y hap-py, I have the love of

Je-sus in my heart, And I'm so hap-py, so ver-y

hap-py, I have the love of Je-sus in my heart.

2. I have the love of Jesus, love of Jesus down in my heart, (where?)
   Down in my heart, (where?) down in my heart,
   I have the love of Jesus, love of Jesus down in my heart, (where?)
   Down in my heart to stay.
   Chorus

3. I have the peace that passeth understanding...
   Chorus

4. I have the wonderful love of my blessed Redeemer way down in the depths of my heart...

REJOICE IN THE LORD ALWAYS

Philippians 4:4 (Round)

Re-joice in the Lord— al——ways and a-gain I

say re-joice! (clap!clap!) Re-joice in the Lord—

al— ways and a-gain I say re-joice! (clap,clap)

Re-joice,— re-joice,— and a-gain I say re-

joice! (clap,clap) Re-joice,— re-joice,— and a-

gain I say re-joice! (clap, clap)

INDEX

*Titles with asterisks are fingerplays which are rhymes illustrated by the use of finger motions.

Discover the entire best-selling line
of Wee Sing® books, audio, and DVDs

Book & CD packages
• Wee Sing Children's Songs and Fingerplays • Wee Sing and Play
• Wee Sing Silly Songs • Wee Sing Sing-Alongs
• Wee Sing for Christmas • Wee Sing Nursery Rhymes and Lullabies
• Wee Sing Bible Songs • Wee Sing America • Wee Sing Fun 'n' Folk
• Wee Sing Dinosaurs • Wee Sing Around the World
• Wee Sing More Bible Songs • Wee Sing for Baby
• Wee Sing Games, Games, Games • Wee Sing in the Car
• Wee Sing Animals, Animals, Animals • Wee Sing and Pretend
• Wee Sing 25th Anniversary Celebration • Wee Sing for Halloween

Board Books
• The Hokey Pokey • Away in a Manger
• The Ten Days of Christmas • The Ants Go Marching
• If You're Happy and You Know It • Old MacDonald

Wee Sing® & Learn Board Book & CD packages
• Wee Sing & Learn ABC • Wee Sing & Learn 123
• Wee Sing & Learn COLORS • Wee Sing & Learn DINOSAURS

Live-Action DVDs
• Wee Sing Together • Wee Sing King Cole's Party
• Wee Sing Grandpa's Magical Toys
• Wee Sing in Sillyville • Wee Sing the Best Christmas Ever!
• Wee Sing in the Big Rock Candy Mountains
• Wee Sing in the Marvelous Musical Mansion
• The Wee Sing Train • Wee Sing Under the Sea

**Wee Sing® products are available
wherever children's books and toys are sold.**